Might goes hand in hand with right as He-Man and the Masters of the Universe fight to make their planet safe. The greatest of their enemies is Skeletor, the Lord of Destruction, and his evil band, whose hatred for their foes is never-ending. The war goes on but who will win?

British Library Cataloguing in Publication Data

Grant, John, *1930-*
    He-Man and the lost dragon. —
    (Masters of the universe)
    I. Title   II. Davies, Robin, *1950-*
    III. Series
    823'.914[J]   PZ7
    ISBN 0-7214-0983-0

First edition

Published by Ladybird Books Ltd Loughborough Leicestershire UK
Ladybird Books Inc Lewiston Maine 04240 USA

MASTERS
OF THE UNIVERSE™

He-Man and the
Lost Dragon

by John Grant
illustrated by Robin Davies

Ladybird Books

In his fortress in the middle of the Fright
Zone, Hordak planned once again to defeat
Skeletor. He called the members of the Horde to
a council of war.

"Skeletor is cunning," he said. "We must find
a way to attack him that will be a complete
surprise. I want ideas."

Grizzlor bared his teeth. "I have heard," he
grunted, "that there is a place on Eternia that is
the home of great monsters. If we were to turn
them loose, Skeletor *and* He-Man would be too
busy fighting them off to notice the Horde until
it was too late."

"Show me," said Hordak, pointing to a map of planet Eternia.

"There," said Grizzlor, pointing. "In the Mystic Mountains. It is called the Lost Valley. The mountains are so high that the monsters can't escape."

"We will give them a helping hand," said Hordak with an evil laugh. "We should be kind to animals!"

A few days later, a sinister space cruiser orbited Eternia. At the controls, Hordak steered a course which brought the cruiser high above the Mystic Mountains. At the observation window, Mantenna kept a sharp look-out. Then he cried, "There it is. Exactly as it is shown on the map!"

Other members of the Horde crowded to look. Far below was a wide, deep valley. Mountains rose steeply on all sides.

"The Lost Valley!" exclaimed Grizzlor. "But I don't see any monsters!"

"We are too far above to see anything," said Hordak. "Let us not waste time. Prepare the vibrobomb for launching."

It was late evening when Hordak's space cruiser was in position over the foot-hills of the Mystic Mountains. "Release the vibrobomb!" he ordered.

From the bomb hatch of the cruiser the
rocket-powered bomb dropped away. The Horde
watched as it disappeared from view. Then,
there came a loud rumble from the surface of
the planet. Cracks ran swiftly along the ground
and over the hills. And a huge section of the
mountains surrounding the Lost Valley collapsed
in a cloud of dust.

"Now," cried Hordak with an evil laugh, "we shall see what horrors make their way out of the Valley. Skeletor and He-Man are going to be very busy. We will wait until they least expect it, then we will attack."

"It won't be a surprise if they see our ship," said Mantenna.

"That is why we are going into hiding," said Hordak. "Set a course for the asteroid cluster. We will orbit under cover of one of the asteroids, and watch everything that happens on Eternia. I will choose my moment."

*   *   *

The shock-waves from Hordak's vibrobomb spread swiftly across Eternia. Farms and villages were destroyed. There was damage to the Royal Palace, many miles away.

King Randor sent for his councillors. "Your Majesty, it seems there has been an earthquake," they reported. "Buildings have been destroyed, and many people have been hurt."

The king put his son, Prince Adam, in charge of the rescue operations. On the way, Adam changed into He-Man, to help with his great strength. He-Man and his helpers worked hard, and by the end of a week people had been rescued from the ruins, doctors were tending the injured, and houses were being rebuilt. He-Man changed back into Adam, and returned to the palace.

Then, a messenger came from a far-off village. The village had been completely destroyed — but not by the earthquake. A huge dragon had come and knocked the village flat!

The king and council laughed. Everyone knew that there were no such things as dragons. They asked the messenger to describe the creature.

"It is ten times the size of a grown man," he said, "with a long, spiked tail."

"Does it breathe fire?" the king asked with a smile.

"No," said the messenger. "It just knocks things down, and frightens the people."

11

The councillors roared with laughter again.
But even as they did, word came of another
dragon, and another. Or perhaps it was the
same dragon in different places. It had eaten
the crops in the fields, as well as most of the
trees in the nearby forest. It seemed that there
really was a dragon loose on Eternia.

"The army will soon take care of it," said the
king.

"Wait," cried Prince Adam. "I should like to
know more about this dragon before we decide.
I have some questions to ask the messengers."

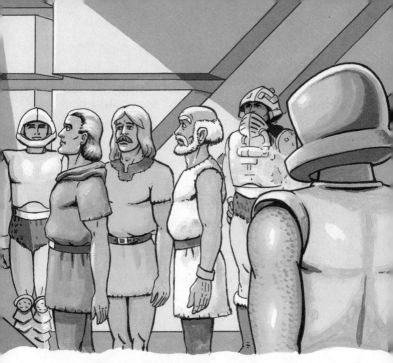

"Very well," said the king.

"Tell me," said the prince, "has the dragon hurt anyone?"

"No," said one man, "but it turned nasty when we tried to drive it away with sticks."

"I'm not surprised," said Adam. "How about the village it destroyed? And the crops? And the forest?"

"Oh, it tried to walk down a narrow village street," said the man. "And it ate the corn and the trees because it was hungry, I suppose."

Adam turned to the king. "My guess," he said, "is that the dragon is a very big, hungry and frightened animal. It was disturbed by the earthquake, I reckon. I think we should find it and help it to return from where it came."

"Very well," said the king. "I give you a week. If by that time the dragon is not gone... then we will have to get rid of it."

Prince Adam left the Royal Palace. "This is a task for the Masters of the Universe," he said. He drew the Sword of Power, and with a cry of:

"BY THE POWER OF GRAYSKULL!"

he became He-Man, Mightiest Man in the Universe.

Quickly he made his way to Castle Grayskull. An electronic map showed immediately where the earthquake had happened. A search in the ancient books of the castle library gave him an idea of what sort of creature the dragon was.

Then he sent for his comrades, the Masters of the Universe.

"From the descriptions I have heard," He-Man told them, "the dragon is a stegosaurus. They have long since vanished from Eternia... except in one place."

"The Mystic Mountains!" said Teela.

"Exactly," said He-Man. "That is where the earthquake was worst. There must be a break in the mountain wall, and the stegosaurus has escaped. We have a week to find it and return it to its home."

"I've heard of the stegosaurus," said Man-at-Arms. "They were very gentle creatures."

"They were also very stupid," said Teela. "Which may not make our task any easier."

* * *

In a fleet of Wind Raiders, the Masters of the Universe headed for the village where the dragon had been last seen. It was still there. A crowd of villagers carrying sticks, scythes and pitch-forks surrounded it at a safe distance.

As the Wind Raiders landed on the village green, the stegosaurus turned slowly to watch them. It looked angry.

"I think that it's hungry," said the Head Villager "But it has already eaten everything for miles around."

Teela raised her Kobra staff and sent out a thought signal to the creature. There was no reply. But she remembered how stupid these animals were supposed to be, and she tried again. This time she caught a faint thought from the enormous beast: "FRIGHTENED!"

Then, she heard: "HUNGRY!"

"It is frightened and hungry," said Teela.

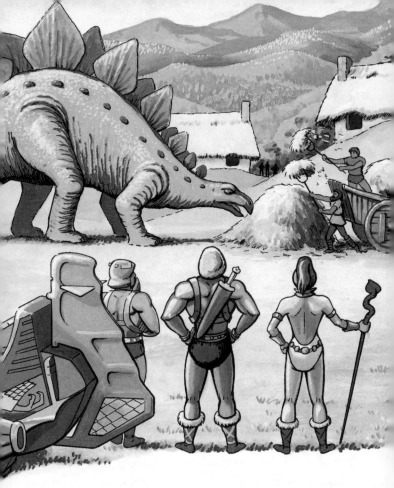

Cartloads of hay were brought from all the
outlying farms. When the stegosaurus had eaten
the last piece, it lay down and fell asleep.

"Now," said He-Man, "we must plan how we
are to get it home to the Mystic Mountains."

Meanwhile, far away in Snake Mountain,
Skeletor screamed at his slaves. The last
vibrations from Hordak's missile had reached
Skeletor's lair. Parts of the ramparts had been
shaken down, and the slaves were toiling hard to
repair them.

One of Skeletor's spies reported to him. "My
lord," he cried, "the Masters of the Universe
have a strange and awful creature. They
doubtless plan to use it against you!"

In his secret control room, Skeletor gazed at the screen of the video spy-scan. He saw the Masters of the Universe standing near the village. He also saw the stegosaurus.

"What a beauty!" he exclaimed. "With such a creature under my control, everyone would obey me. Anyone who did not would be trampled flat!"

He ordered his Roton to be made ready. It would be easy to snatch such a prize from He-Man and his stupid friends!

While He-Man made plans to save the stegosaurus, and Skeletor prepared to steal it, Hordak was growing impatient.

"Where are all the monsters?" he raged. "You said that the Lost Valley was filled with monsters! We have wasted time and a vibrobomb!"

"We must be patient," said Grizzlor.

"I have no time to be patient!" shouted Hordak. And he ordered one of his imps into a scout capsule to find out what was happening.

When he returned from his mission to the
planet's surface, the imp reported, "Only one
monster has come out of the mountains. The
Masters of the Universe are guarding it. I saw
no sign of Skeletor."

"I think that it is time that I took charge of
proceedings," said Hordak. "Prepare for a
landing on planet Eternia!"

He-Man had almost completed his
preparations for returning the stegosaurus to its
home. Stratos had flown high over the
mountains, and had seen the gap through which
the monster had escaped. He told the others,
"The fastest route will take us across a swift
river, but that river flows in a deep gorge. The
only way across is by a rock arch which may not
be strong enough for such a heavy load."

Man-at-Arms flew back to Castle Grayskull.
He returned with what he called his Dragon-
Catching Kit. The first piece of equipment was
a neuro-transducer. "We fix it to the

stegosaurus' head with these suction cups," he explained. "Teela will then be able to speak to it by thought waves."

"Let's fix it while the animal is asleep," said He-Man. He climbed on to the scaly back, and inched his way along the neck towards the head. He had just fitted the device... when the stegosaurus woke! With an angry roar, it shook itself, and He-Man was sent flying through the air! He landed with a thump!

Teela called out, "It's working! I'm getting thought signals! And it's very, very angry at you, He-Man!"

Teela managed to calm the huge creature.

"It's time that we made a start," said He-Man. "From what Stratos has said, we should be able to make the whole trip through forest. That way we will be out of sight of possible enemies. More important, the stegosaurus will have plenty to eat."

The villagers gathered to see the stegosaurus on its way.

Teela sent out thought waves, "We are your friends. We will lead you home to the Mystic Mountains."

And Teela heard in her mind the thoughts of the stegosaurus, "FRIENDS... ...HOME!"

Teela led the way in a Wind Raider. She hovered close to the ground in front of the stegosaurus, which plodded along behind her.

The villagers cheered. The stegosaurus turned its head. From its simple mind Teela caught the thought, "GOODBYE, FRIENDS!"

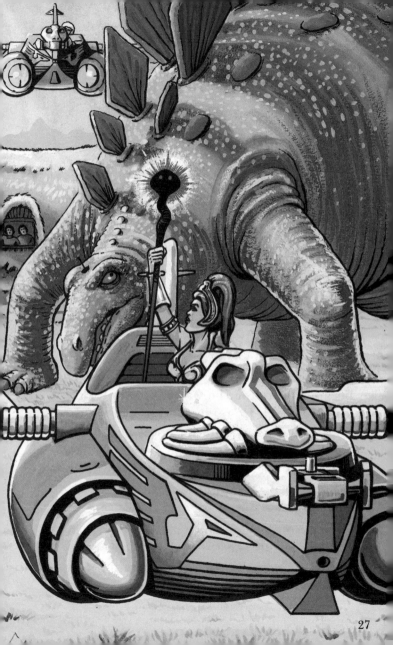

High in the sky, Stratos watched his comrades
set out with the giant animal. His task was to
keep a look-out for any trouble. He quickly
became aware that he was not the only one
keeping watch from the air. Far away and below
Stratos saw a small moving speck. From the
cover of a patch of cloud he flew close. The
object was one of Skeletor's evil hover machines,
a Roton, with the Lord of Destruction himself at
the controls.

The Roton came no closer. Skeletor was
keeping his distance from the Masters of the
Universe. Whatever he planned to do, he was in
no hurry.

* * *

Skeletor watched the sensors on the Roton. Something was wrong. He already knew where the Masters of the Universe were, and what they were doing. But now he was picking up a signal that he did not understand. Some large craft had landed and was hidden not very far away. It must be an enemy. Had the Masters of the Universe friends he didn't know about? Or, was someone planning to steal the dragon before he did?

Hordak led the members of the Horde from
the space cruiser, where it lay hidden in the
foot-hills of the Mystic Mountains. Weapons at
the ready, they advanced. Mantenna went ahead
as scout. Grizzlor prowled along, looking for signs
on the ground that would tell him if an enemy
were close. Suddenly, Modulok held up his hand.
"I sense the presence of a large reptile," he said.
"Some kilometres distant. Over that way."

Leech moved forward in his turn. "Yes," he grunted. "There is a great reptile not far away. And enemies too!"

"Forward!" cried Hordak, and the evil company made its way swiftly towards the distant stegosaurus and its guardians, the Masters of the Universe.

The stegosaurus travelled very slowly. It stopped often to eat and sleep. Teela tried to explain to it that it had less than a week to get safely back to its valley. But it was too stupid to understand.

Then one morning, they saw the peaks of the Mystic Mountains. They were now only a short distance from the rock arch over the river. He-Man and Man-at-Arms walked on ahead to examine it. The arch was cracked and crumbling. "We're going to cross on *that*?" exclaimed Man-at-Arms.

He-Man took a few steps on to the arch. Pieces of rock broke away and dropped into the gorge. "We must hurry," he said. "It won't stand much longer."

They walked back to Teela and the stegosaurus. It had stopped feeding, and was standing with its head raised as if it were listening. The neuro-transducer was picking up thought waves. Evil thought waves.

Under cover of the forest, Skeletor lay hidden, planning his next move.

Skeletor had another look at the stegosaurus. "One stun-blast from the Roton's laser cannon will put it to sleep," he said to himself. "Then I can deal with those interfering Masters of the Universe."

He set the Roton to rise gently above the tree-tops. Now he had a clear view of the monster. When the right moment came, he would be ready to strike.

*   *   *

Skeletor's thought waves had made the stegosaurus nervous. But when it saw the high, narrow rock arch it grew more nervous still. It took one look and refused to move. Man-at-Arms took a short metal rod out of his Wind Raider. "It's part of my Dragon-Catching Kit," he said. "An energy noose." He pressed a switch, and a beam of light shot out. He pressed another switch and the light formed a loop. He dropped the loop over Teela's shoulders, and it held her firmly but gently.

Teela took the rod and put the loop around the neck of the stegosaurus. She tugged gently, and the stegosaurus followed. Slowly she led it on to the rock arch.

"Now!" cried Skeletor. "While they are busy with their pet!" And he launched the Roton on an attack course.

But even as he did so, a storm of fire from energy weapons crashed around him. He dived for the cover of the trees and there he saw a new enemy!

"Hordak!" cried Skeletor. "How dare you meddle in my affairs! There is no room for both of us on Eternia!"

"Right!" shouted Hordak. "And you will be wise to step aside for me!"

"Never!" screamed Skeletor. And he swung the Roton to attack Hordak.

The noise of battle brought the Masters of the Universe running. Leaving Hordak to deal with Skeletor, Modulok led the rest of the Horde in an attack on the Masters. The stegosaurus was almost half-way across the arch. It stopped and looked back. It must help its new friends. It backed off the arch to solid ground. It could see Modulok fighting furiously. Teela heard the creature's thoughts, "I can fight too." Next moment it swung its enormous, spiked tail. The warriors of the Horde were scattered in all directions.

"Quick!" cried He-Man. "Over the arch before they recover."

This time the stegosaurus was persuaded to hurry. It reached the far side just as the evil warriors returned to the attack, led by Grizzlor. They rushed on to the rock arch. The stegosaurus stopped and looked back, annoyed by their evil thought waves. It took a step forward and put one giant foot on the arch. Then it pushed!

Grizzlor felt the rock tremble under his feet. He stopped, and Mantenna crashed into him. The whole company, Grizzlor, Mantenna, Modulok, tumbled in a heap. Leech tried to hang on with his suction discs, but the arch was already swaying from side to side. The stegosaurus gave one last heave, and the rock arch and the warriors of the Horde vanished into the gorge. The Masters of the Universe ran to the edge in time to see their enemies land with a splash in the river far below.

"Getting out of that will keep them busy for some time," said He-Man.

Once again, Teela led the stegosaurus towards the Mystic Mountains. Soon it would be home in the Lost Valley.

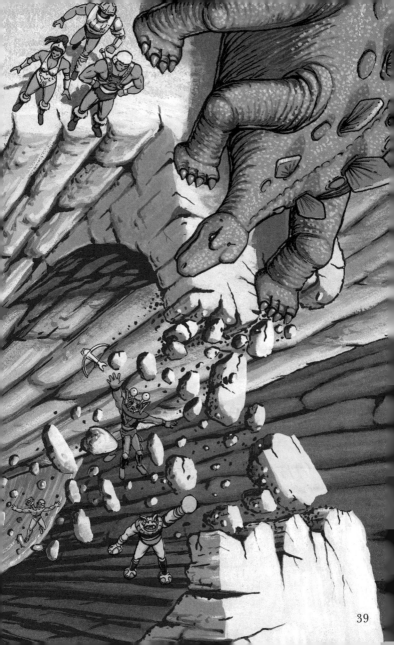

At the sound of the rock arch falling into the gorge, Skeletor broke off his fight with Hordak. With Hordak still firing at him, he swooped over the river. He saw the stegosaurus plodding along.

"Those meddlers are still trying to rob me!" he shrieked. He came racing in, laser cannons firing. The Masters of the Universe dived for cover, firing their own weapons, trying to protect the stegosaurus.

The stegosaurus stood still. "ANOTHER ONE!" came the thought from its simple mind. It waited for a moment. Then as Skeletor whirled in for another attack, it swung its mighty tail. The spikes hit the Roton and knocked it out of control! The damaged machine zigzagged back across the gorge. It flipped on to its back, and Skeletor was thrown out. He landed high in the branches of a tall tree, and watched as the Roton careered over the edge of the gorge and vanished into the river.

There was no sign of Hordak anywhere.

Late in the day, the Masters of the Universe reached the Mystic Mountains. And there, straight ahead, was the gap made by Hordak's vibrobomb. The stegosaurus began to walk faster.

Teela led it through the gap. Beyond was a mysterious, misty valley. Teela reached up and patted the huge creature. "You're home," she said. In her mind she heard, "HOME. GOOD."

The stegosaurus made its way down the valley. He-Man hurried after it. "You won't need this any more," he said. And he climbed up and took the neuro-transducer from the animal's head. As he did so, the Masters of the Universe caught one last thought wave from the giant creature, "GOODBYE... ...FRIENDS!" Then it was gone, into the mist of the Lost Valley.

There was a sound of powerful engines overhead. An evil-looking craft hovered above them. Hordak!

He-Man and the others raced for the shelter of the rocks, as Hordak fired at them with all the power his craft could muster. He had one vibrobomb left. He launched it. But the Masters of the Universe were already on their Wind Raiders and out of range. The missile struck the mountainside. The rocks crashed down with a noise like thunder into the gap. The Lost Valley was sealed once more.

"Never fear," roared Hordak, as he went off in search of his Horde. "I will be back!"

"And we will be ready!" cried the Masters of the Universe together.